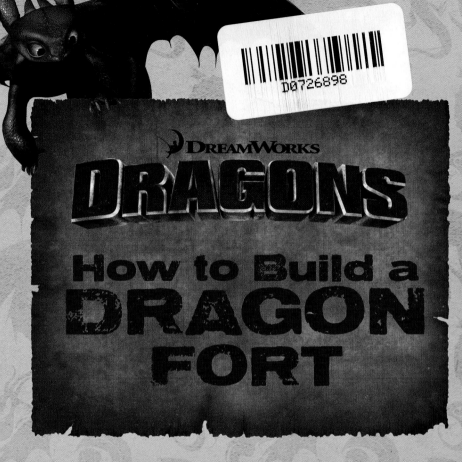

DREAMWORKS

DRAGONS

How to Build a DRAGON FORT

adapted by Erica David

HODDER CHILDREN'S BOOKS

First published by Simon Spotlight
An imprint of Simon & Schuster Children's Publishing Division
1230 Avenue of the Americas, New York, New York 10020

First published in Great Britain in 2017 by Hodder and Stoughton

DreamWorks Dragons © 2017 DreamWorks Animation LLC.

A CIP catalogue record for this book
is available from the British Library.

ISBN 978 1 444 93429 8

Printed and bound in China by RR Donnelley Asia Printing Solutions Limited

The paper and board used in this book are made from wood from responsible sources

MIX
Paper from
responsible sources
FSC® C104740

Hodder Children's Books
An imprint of
Hachette Children's Group
Part of Hodder and Stoughton
Carmelite House
50 Victoria Embankment
London EC4Y 0DZ

An Hachette UK Company
www.hachette.co.uk

www.hachettechildrens.co.uk

Hiccup and his friends were on a mission.

They wanted to find the perfect place to build an island outpost for themselves and their dragons.

It would be their dragon fort.

They visited many islands, but none felt right. None felt like home.

And some were even dangerous!

Astrid and her dragon, Stormfly, helped keep the Dragon Riders safe.

Finally they found the right place.
Everyone was excited but they each had
a different idea for the fort.

Snotlout wanted the fort shaped like an S for his name.

Fishlegs wanted a place to relax.

Astrid wanted the fort to be well armed.

Ruffnut and Tuffnut wanted a boar pit.

Hiccup and his dragon, Toothless, didn't know what to do. How could they build a fort to make everyone happy? They decided to sleep on it.

That night Tuffnut heard a strange noise.
He went to see what it was.

In a clearing not far from the camp, Tuffnut watched as a massive dragon rose into the air.

Tuffnut ran to tell his friends. "We have to get out of here!" he warned them.

But they didn't believe him.
"Is anyone falling for this?" asked Astrid.

"I'm not making it up!" said Tuffnut.

Hiccup, Tuffnut and Ruffnut went to look for the giant dragon.

At first they didn't find anything.
Then they saw a dark shape up ahead.

"I don't believe it!" said Hiccup.

The giant dragon roared and flew off.
It was headed for their camp! Snotlout,
Fishlegs and Astrid were in danger!

Hiccup, Tuffnut and Ruffnut chased the giant dragon. Then Tuffnutt and Ruffnut flew right through it!

"It's not one big dragon," Hiccup pointed out. "It's tons of little ones!" The little dragons flew in a group. Together they looked like one big dragon!

The little dragons had a leader. He was small and white.
Tuffnut and Ruffnut captured him!

Back at the camp, Fishlegs named the little dragons Night Terrors.

The little white Night Terror wasn't happy. He wanted to get back to the other Night Terrors.

Without their leader the Night Terrors were in trouble! They were under attack from two scary Changewings!

Hiccup and his friends flew to the rescue!

They fought the Changewings to protect the Night Terrors. But they were outnumbered!

The Night Terrors needed their leader!

"They flock into the shape of a giant version of themselves as a defence to scare off predators," Fishlegs pointed out.

"Without their leader they can't!" Hiccup said.

Hiccup zoomed back to the camp. He released the white Night Terror and the little dragon flew off to join the battle.

The Changewings chased the white Night Terror.

They were closing in when Hiccup, Toothless, and the other dragons and their riders saved him!

The white Night Terror joined the rest of his flock. They all came together in the shape of a huge dragon!

The Changewings were scared of the big dragon! They shrieked and ran away!

Hiccup and his friends cheered.

The next morning Hiccup showed his friends a plan for the fort.

"I got the idea from the Night Terrors," Hiccup said. "I combined all your ideas into one giant base!"

"We can call it the Dragon's Edge,"
said Hiccup. "Astrid, you can make your
section heavily armed!"

"Fishlegs, your place is quiet and relaxing,"
Hiccup explained.

"Snotlout, your spot isn't S-shaped,"
Hiccup said. "But you can paint
as many *S*'s as you like!"

"Ruffnut and Tuffnut, you can even have a boar pit," Hiccup told the twins.

Everyone loved Hiccup's plan.

A few days later Dragon's Edge was complete.

"And now for one more addition," Hiccup announced.

The white Night Terror landed on a perch beside Hiccup. "The Night Terrors will be our lookouts!" he explained.

Then the Night Terrors flocked together.
High in the sky they formed a dragon
shaped just like Toothless!

Toothless snorted proudly. There was nothing like new friends to make Dragon's Edge feel like home.